MINTLAW

KV-512-252

Captain Jones's Bones

ORCHARD BOOKS
96 Leonard Street, London EC2A 4RH
Orchard Books Australia
14 Mars Road, Lane Cove, NSW 2066
ISBN 1 86039 154 0 (hardback)
ISBN 1 86039 324 1 (paperback)
First published in Great Britain in 1996
First paperback publication 1997
Text and illustrations © Ross Thomson 1996
The right of Ross Thomson to be identified as
the author and illustrator of this work has been
asserted by him in accordance with the
Copyright, Designs and Patents Act, 1988.
A CIP catalogue record for this book is
available from the British Library.
Printed in Great Britain

Captain Jones's Bones

Written and Illustrated
by Ross Thomson

ORCHARD BOOKS

Captain Jones and his crew were
the worst and poorest pirates to
sail the seven seas.

The crew were not very
happy.

When they reached home after another long voyage, the ship was quite empty.

Once again, they had not found any treasure at all.

The people from the town came
to the harbour to laugh at the
pirates.

They all had great fun.

While Captain Jones went to the
chart shop, the crew went to the
Inn.

"We mustn't give up," said Captain Jones. "I'm off to make plans for our next voyage."

"I need a new chart – one that will find us some treasure!" he said to the shopkeeper, who invited him to stay for tea.

12

"Try this chart book," said the shopkeeper, "it's just come in. They say it used to belong to a very famous pirate."

Captain Jones studied one of the charts. He felt very excited.

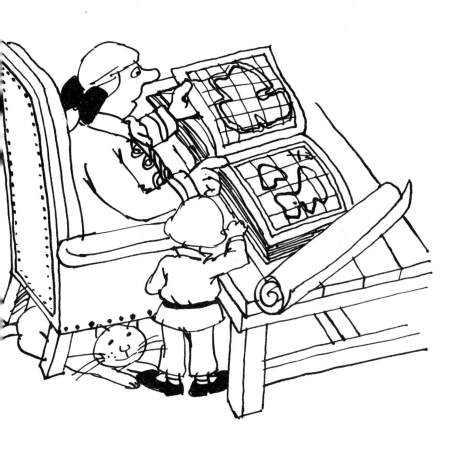

He turned the pages of the book.
He hadn't visited any of these
islands before.

Then, as he turned to the next page, he noticed an old map, tucked inside.

It could only mean one thing –
treasure!

He ran down the hill to tell his crew.

Now they would be rich. But. . .

"I've heard all this before," said the First Mate.

"He's right! He's right!" squawked the Cockatoo.

"I'm fed up," said the Bosun

"I feel down," said the Second Mate

"We don't want to go,"
said the Navigator.

"It'll be just like last
time," groaned
the Cook.

But the Cabin Boy said,
"Oh, please let's go!"

When the ship sailed out of the
harbour on the next tide, the
crew were sulking.

They sailed for many days until
they reached an island.

"Land Ho!" shouted the First
Mate.

"Land Ho!" squawked the
Cockatoo.

Everyone climbed into the
dinghy, and they rowed ashore.

"This way" pointed Captain
Jones excitedly, as he followed
the map.

The crew followed behind grumbling.

"Are we there yet," moaned the First Mate.

"This way! This way!" squawked the Cockatoo.

" This is the spot! Start digging!" said Captain Jones excitedly.

"Only if you say *please!*" grumbled the Cook.

The crew took it in turns to dig.
After many hours they hit
something solid.

"It must be the treasure!"
shouted the Cabin Boy.

Captain Jones jumped up and
down with glee.

But when the they pulled out the
treasure. . .

"It's just a large bone," said the First Mate.

"And another!" said the Bosun.

"And these look like ribs!" said the Second Mate.

"I've got two more," said the Navigator.

"I can't even make soup from this bone," said the Cook.

"I think we have a bone to pick with the Captain," said the Cabin Boy.

"Please keep digging," said Captain Jones, "Maybe the treasure is further down."

But the pile of old bones just got bigger and bigger.

"What a waste of time!" said the crew. They were very angry and wanted to go back to the ship and sail home.

"Wait!" said the Cabin Boy.
"These aren't just any old bones,
these are. . . Dinosaur Bones!"

40

Suddenly Captain Jones was smiling. "I think I've got an idea that will make us rich after all!" he said.

When Captain Jones and his crew returned with lovely new clothes and a freshly painted ship, the townspeople did not laugh at them.

"Did you find treasure after all?" asked the Mayor.

"We certainly did! " said
Captain Jones.

Pirate Facts

Blackbeard is one of the most famous pirates. He made himself look even more scarey by lighting fuses and putting them in his ears, so that thick black smoke seemed to billow out from his head.

Each pirate ship had a slightly different Jolly Roger flag, as the captain usually designed his own.

There were several famous women pirates, such as Anne Bonny and Mary Read.

Most pirates who were caught were hanged, but those who weren't had a letter 'P' burned onto their forehead.

Beetle and Bug

and the
Pharaoh's Tomb

Hiawyn Oram
Illustrated by Sonia Holleyman

N E S L S

1092711

JS

109271l

ORCHARD BOOKS

96 Leonard Street, London EC2A 4RH

Orchard Books Australia

14 Mars Road, Lane Cove, NSW 2066

ISBN 1 85213 890 4 (hardback)

ISBN 1 86039 016 1 (paperback)

First published in Great Britain 1995

First paperback publication 1996

Text © Hiawyn Oram 1995

Illustrations © Sonia Holleyman 1995

The right of Hiawyn Oram to be identified as the author
and Sonia Holleyman as the illustrator of this work has been
asserted by them in accordance with the Copyright,
Designs and Patents Act, 1988.

A CIP catalogue record for this book is available from the British Library.

Printed in Great Britain by Guernsey Press, C.I.